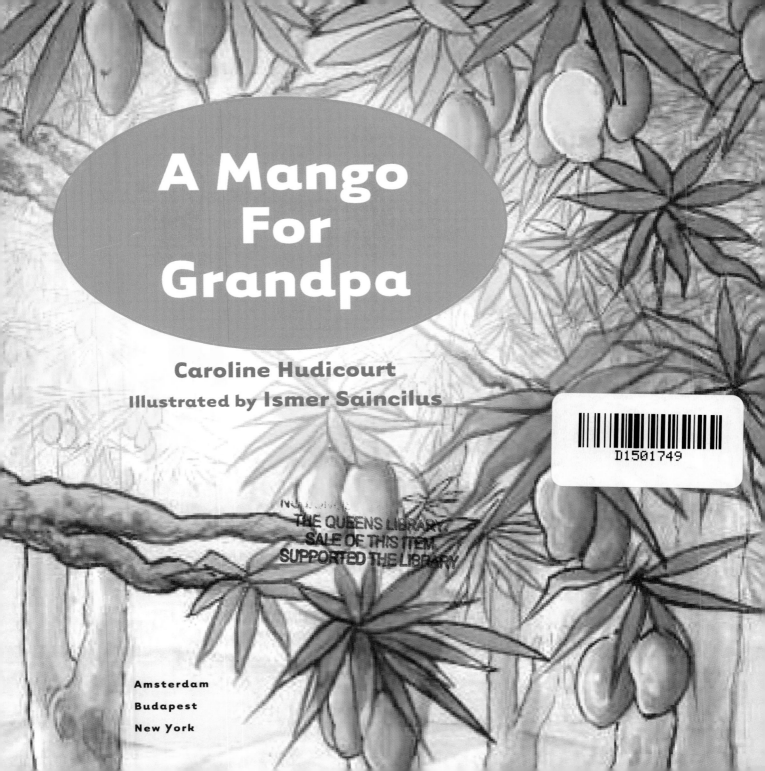

A Mango For Grandpa

Caroline Hudicourt

Illustrated by Ismer Saincilus

Amsterdam

Budapest

New York

This is a publication of the Reading Corner project of
International Step By Step Association
Keizersgracht 62–64
1015 CS Amsterdam
The Netherlands
www.issa.nl

ISBN 978-1-931854-51-1

PRINTED IN U.S.A.

I dedicate this story to my
father, Georges Hudicourt,
whose generous and gregarious
personality shines through in
every page of *A Mango for
Grandpa,* and to my children,
Jessica and Anais, who have
helped me see his aging years
with youthful eyes.

—C.H.

The International Step by Step Association (ISSA) promotes quality care and education for each child based on democratic values, child-centered approaches, active parent and community involvement, and a commitment to diversity and inclusion. ISSA advances its mission by informing, educating and supporting individuals who influence the lives of children. ISSA advocates for effective policies, develops standards, advances research and evidenced based practices, provides opportunities for professional development and strengthens global alliances. For more information see our website at www.issa.nl.

Whenever I eat a mango, I still think of Grandpa...

Beep beep beep beeeeep!

"Grandpa is here!" We'd all run out to meet him.

"Come and see the mangoes I've brought!" he'd yell proudly as he got out of his car.

Five of us grandchildren would race out to help carry the mangoes.

With twenty-seven grandchildren, Grandpa never had trouble finding help.

We'd sit together around the kitchen table, cutting and biting into the thick, juicy, sweet fruits.

"There is no country in the world where you could find better mangoes," Grandpa would tell us.

Grandpa and mangoes always brightened our day.

Once he picked some of us up after school and took us to buy mangoes. He stopped next to a street merchant and her donkey, with two large bags of fruit on its back.

Grandpa asked: "How much is the donkey?"

The merchant said, "I've had people buy mangoes by the dozen, but never by the donkey!"

We all laughed.

Grandpa always loved to see his house full of kids, and when we visited, he always found reasons to call us into the room.

"Martiiiine!!! Could you get me a glass of water, please?"

"Yes, Grandpa," my sister would say from upstairs.

A few minutes later, I'd walk through the living room.

"Anaïs, could you get me a glass of water, please?"

"Yes, Grandpa."

We'd end up fighting in the kitchen.

"Let me get the water first. It's for Grandpa."

"But mine is, too."

Nobody dared say something like "Why don't you get it yourself?" to grandpa.

We knew he worked very hard, seeing forty to sixty patients a day. When he got home he had the right to be waited on.

When we didn't want to run an errand for him, we'd tiptoe through the living room so he wouldn't notice we were around.

He often got our names wrong. He called Martine "Anaïs," or Valerie "Monica," or Louis-Gary "Patrice".

We thought it was so funny.

Then, one day, we realized he wasn't getting the names confused: he didn't remember our names at all.

We stopped laughing.

Soon he didn't know where he was. "I want to go home," he'd say.

"You are already home," I would say as I put my hand on his bald head.

By then, Grandpa couldn't go out by himself anymore. He could not buy us mangoes.

"What's wrong with Grandpa?" I asked Grandma Edith.

"His old brain is sick," she answered. "He took care of us for a long time, now we have to take care of him."

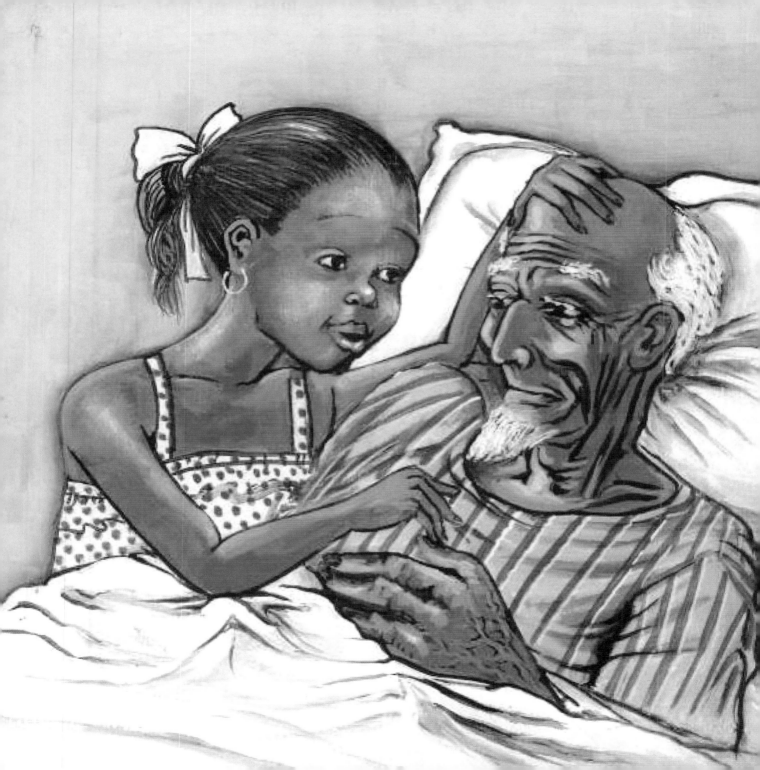

One afternoon, on the way home from school, I noticed some mango trees by the side of the road. I decided to pick some fruit for Grandpa.

I knew how to climb the small guava tree, but I'd never climbed the tall mango tree before.

I climbed up the trunk of one of the smallest trees. The ground looked so incredibly far away. I was afraid but I kept climbing.

I crawled out on a branch, stretched one arm as far as I could towards the best-looking mango, and opened my hand wide.

My heart pounded with excitement. It didn't matter how high up in the air I was any more, all that mattered was to get that mango for grandpa.

I grabbed it and pulled it. I had it! I felt so proud.

I ran to my grandparents' house.

"Here, Grandpa! Look what I brought you!"

"Thank you!!! That's one of the most beautiful mangoes I've ever seen," he said.

I felt happy and kind of powerful. Grandpa stood up, went to the kitchen, and cut and ate the mango all by himself.

After that, I brought him a mango every day.

One day, he seemed to have a hard time cutting it, but he didn't ask for help. I helped him anyway.

"Thank you." He said it very humbly, as I heard him say it to Grandma Edith several times a day.

Soon I had to feed him the mango with a spoon. He stopped looking happy and often sang a song I had never heard before. He must have learned it when he was little.

"God, I have nothing to offer you,
But a heart tired of suffering.
As I am, as I am,
My only belonging is my misery."

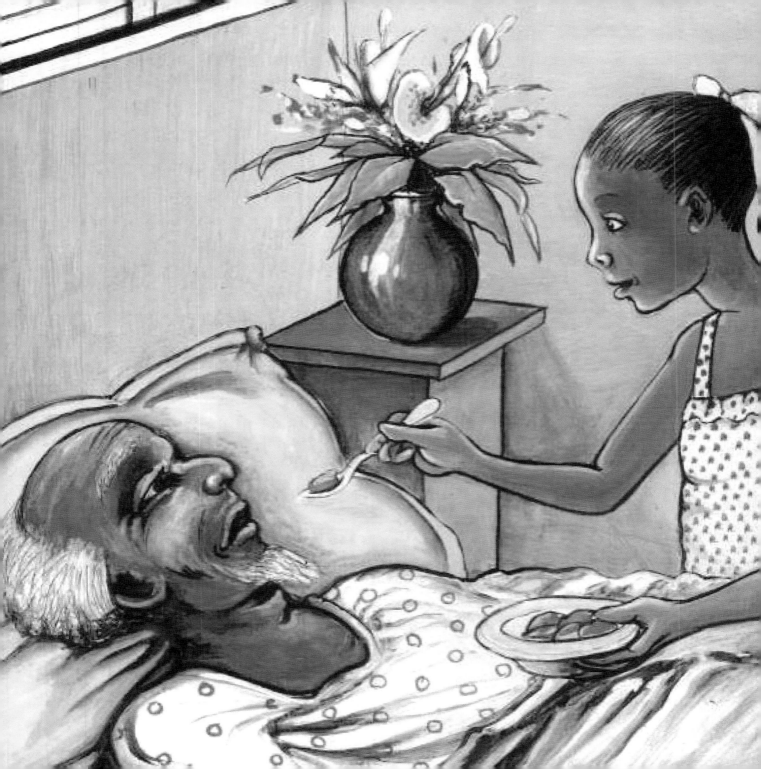

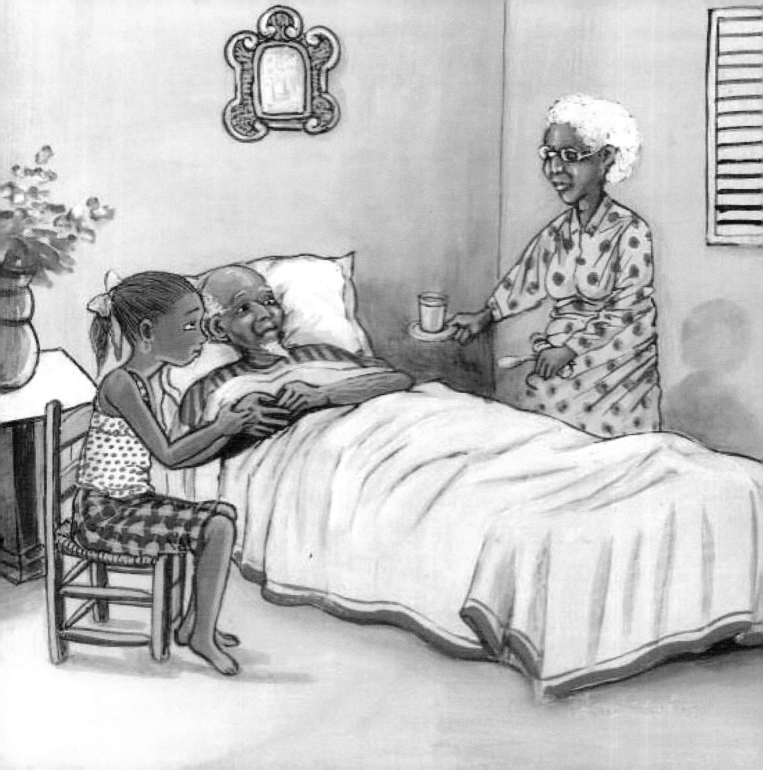

Eventually, he couldn't eat the mangoes I brought anymore; they made him sick. He had great trouble swallowing. I stopped feeding him. Grandma Edith took care of it.

I could still hold his hand, though.

He was slowly leaving us. And he wanted to go. Life had become too painful to him.

Then, one day at school, I was called to the principal's office. As soon as I saw her face, I could tell something was wrong.

"Your mother called. She is going to pick you up and take you to your grandparents' house, because your grandfather just passed away."

I felt sad but relieved. Although I knew I would miss him, I knew he had to go.

For his funeral, we surrounded his coffin with fruit: mangoes, pineapples, oranges, and more.

"How will Grandpa manage to eat all of this?" my little sister Jessica asked.

"He doesnt need to,"– I answered. "We just want to let him know that we love him. It is a gift of love, food for the heart."

After the funeral, we all shared the fruit.

And now, every time we bite into a mango, we think of him.

4541713

Made in the USA
Charleston, SC
08 February 2010